LORD OF THE BEARS

Sandy

Cobby

The Bear Facts

Alice in Bearland

Pebbles

Philpo

For Paddy, Tom, Jack and Leon.

First published in 2004 by The Bear Shop Book Co.,
an imprint of Emma Treehouse Ltd.,
Old Brewhouse, Shepton Mallet BA4 5QE
Text and illustrations copyright © 2004 by Rikey Austin
ISBN 1 85576 415 6
Printed in China
2 4 6 8 10 9 7 5 3 1

Tat

Gets a Patch

Rikey Austin

The Bear Shop Book Co.

Alice and her mum were famous in their town, for mending teddy bears. From all around children (and grown-ups) brought poorly bears, knowing Alice and her mum would mend them and that, mysteriously, the bears would come home somehow happier. No one knew, but this was because when Alice talked to bears, the bears talked back.

So when a bear was upset or miserable, Alice could find out why, and do something to make them better.

There were so many bears to mend that Alice and her mum had opened a bear shop and a special Hospital for Poorly Bears.

Alice was particularly proud of the shop sign, because the shop sign read:

ar Shop

(Hospital for Poorly Bears)

s
for

ed.

Very early one morning a little boy stepped into Alice's Bear Shop.

"My name is Leon," he said.

"This," he said, swinging a much-loved-to-bits bear up into the air by one leg, "is Tat. His stuffing is falling out. Can you mend him, please?"

Tat left a small trail of fluff floating in the air every time Leon swung him about.

The lady behind the counter was Alice's
mum. She took the bear and looked at him
carefully. "Yes, we can make him better," she
said. "Come back in a couple of days and
he'll be as good as new."

Not long after, Alice walked in.
The large brass bell over the door rang loudly.
Alice's mum popped her head out of the
bear hospital at the back of the shop. "Come
and see this, Alice."

On the large wooden table under the skylight sat the saddest bear that Alice had ever seen. His stitching was loose and a little pile of stuffing had already leaked from a hole in his tummy.

Her mum picked up the bear gently. "His name's Tat, do you want to have a go at fixing him?"

"Oh, no!" said Alice. "It's too big a job for me." The bell in the shop rang again and Alice's mum went to see who had come in.

"Oh, dear!" said a small voice from the table, Alice turned to see Tat ringing his paws together miserably. "Oh, dear! Oh, dear!" A large tear fell on to his saggy tummy.

"You should try not to cry," said Alice. "It's not a good idea to get your stuffing wet."

"I'm really not sure about this," said Tat.

"Don't worry," said Alice. "Getting fixed doesn't hurt."

"It's not that," he cried, standing up so quickly that more stuffing filled the air, tickling Alice's nose. "Don't you think that a little wear gives me character?" He puffed his chest out and held his head high. The effect was spoilt when even more filling fell from the hole in his tummy. At some point his left eye had been replaced by a small shirt button. This gave his face a sad, lopsided look.

"Oh yes," answered Alice kindly, "the loved-to-bits look is definitely back in but I think you're about to lose all of your stuffing and your ears are hanging by a thread."

"But," cried Tat, "what if my owner, Leon, doesn't recognize me when I'm finished."

Alice smiled kindly.

"Don't worry," she said softly. "Nobody wants to change the way you look, we just need to make sure nothing drops off if you move suddenly."

Tat had to admit that he had been feeling fragile lately, he nodded and gave Alice a worried little smile. "OK," he agreed. "Let's get started."

Alice got to work. She sewed a patch over the hole in Tat's tummy.

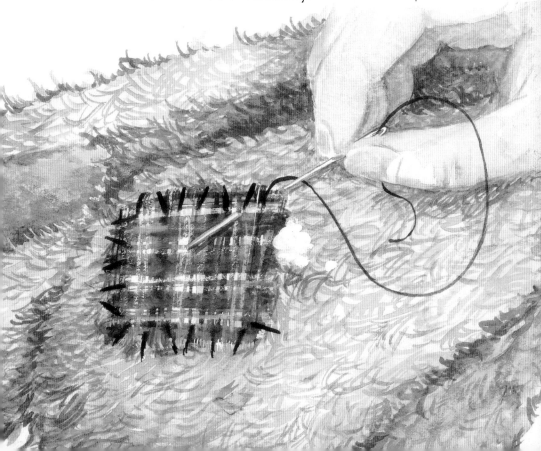

And she stitched his loose ears.

She cleaned him gently and was even able to find a near perfect match for his missing eye.

Finally she lifted a mirror on to the table so that Tat could take a look at himself. He pressed his paws tightly over his eyes and refused to look. "Be brave," said Alice.

Tat peeked between his paws nervously.

"Wow! WOW!" he shouted and then jumped about excitedly.

He stopped suddenly to check his seams and then grinned, "Won't Leon be surprised."

The next morning Alice propped Tat up on a chair by an open door so he could see all the comings and goings in the shop.

The morning wore on, and people came and went, some bringing old bears for repair, others buying one of the many new bears that lived in the shop. Then, suddenly, there was Leon. Tat craned forward with excitement. Leon was stood by the shelves of new bears. He picked one up. Tat's heart fell into his boots.

Tat could hear Leon mutter, "Nice bear!" and watched him stroke its thick, shiny new fur.

"Oh, no," said Tat, but then he heard Leon say to the bear, "I hope Tat's alright, it was horrible sleeping without him last night, I missed him so."

Just then Alice spotted Leon.

"Leon!" she called. "Come and look at Tat! He's all better!"

"I only came in to see him because I missed him so much last night," Leon admitted to Alice as she handed Tat to him.

"He's a very lovely bear," said Alice, as a thrilled Leon left the shop, clutching Tat.

Alice and her mum watched Leon step down the street, dangling a very happy Tat by one arm as he walked.

Alice's mum gave her a huge hug.
"I knew you could do it, Alice, you just had
to be brave."

"Just like Tat." said Alice.

"I hope you used the extra strong thread!" said Alice's mum as Leon and a now wildly swinging Tat disappeared into the crowd.

Paws for Thought!

Seven Brides for Seven Bears

The Thirty-Nine Bears

by Ted E Bear

Tat

Woodroffe

Cooking for Single Bears by Dehlia Bear

BEAR HEROES

T·ing

Icky

Mary-Jane